The Nightingale

Retold by
Michael Bedard

Illustrated by
Regolo Ricci

TORONTO   OXFORD   NEW YORK
OXFORD UNIVERSITY PRESS
1991

Martha My Dear
– M.B.

For Marlena
— R.R.

Oxford University Press, 70 Wynford Drive, Don Mills, Ontario, M3C 1J9

Toronto Oxford New York Delhi Bombay Calcutta Madras Karachi
Petaling Jaya Singapore Hong Kong Tokyo Nairobi Dar es Salaam
Cape Town Melbourne Auckland

and associated companies in
Berlin Ibadan

Canadian Cataloguing in Publication Data
Bedard, Michael, 1949–
The nightingale

ISBN 0–19–540814–4

I. Ricci, Regolo.   II. Title.
PS8553.E39558N53 1991   j398.21   C90–095216–4
PZ8.B433N1 1991

Design: Kathryn Cole

Oxford is a trademark of Oxford University Press
1 2 3 4 — 4 3 2 1

Printed in Hong Kong

*L*ong, long ago there lived an Emperor of China, whose palace was quite the most beautiful palace in the world. It was built entirely of fine porcelain, so brittle that one dared hardly breathe upon it lest it break. His garden was full of wonderful flowers, and to the most beautiful of these were tied small silver bells that tinkled constantly, so that people could not help but notice them as they passed.

So large was the garden that even the gardeners did not know the end of it. But if one kept on walking, one came in time to a wondrous wood with towering trees that swept down as far as the sea. And among the branches of these trees there lived a nightingale.

Now, the sea was so deep and blue near the shore that boats could sail right under the branches of the trees. And the nightingale sang so sweetly there that even the busy fisherman drawing his nets in at night would stop to listen to her.

"So beautiful," he would whisper to himself. "So very beautiful."

Travellers from all the world over came to the Emperor's capital. And though they admired the city and were amazed at the palace and its wonderful garden, when they heard the nightingale sing they all said, "This is the best of all."

The poets among them wrote beautiful poems about all they had seen, but especially of the nightingale that sang in the woods by the sea. Their books went out over the world, until in time one of them reached the hands of the Emperor, who was sitting in the garden on his golden chair. He nodded and nodded, well-pleased with what they had to say of his city and his palace and his wonderful garden.

"But what's this," he cried, "about a nightingale? I know of no nightingale. To think there is such a bird in my kingdom, indeed in my own garden, and I should have to hear of it from a book!"

He called for his Lord Chamberlain.

"They say in this book that there is a wonderful bird in my garden called a nightingale," he said. "In fact, they say that its singing is better than anything else in my kingdom. Why has no one ever mentioned it to me?"

"Forgive me, My Lord, but no one has ever mentioned it to me either."

"It is unthinkable that the world should know of possessions of mine that I know nothing about. I demand that this bird be brought tonight to sing before me. And if it is not here after supper, I shall have everyone at court beaten for it."

"I shall seek and find it, My Lord."

But where should he even begin to look? The Chamberlain ran upstairs and downstairs, through all the halls and rooms of the palace, but no one he spoke to had ever heard of the nightingale. At last, almost out of hope, he came to the kitchen. And when he mentioned the nightingale there, a poor little serving maid stepped forward.

"*S*ir," she said, "each evening, I'm allowed to take scraps from the table to my poor, sick mother who lives down by the seashore. Sometimes on the way back, if I am tired, I rest awhile in the woods. That is where I have heard the nightingale sing, and its song is so sweet it brings tears to my eyes."

"Little serving maid," said the Chamberlain, "I will see that you are given a permanent place in the palace kitchen and permission to see the Emperor himself dining, if you will take me to the nightingale. For it must appear in court this very night."

So they went together to the place in the woods by the sea, and half the court went with them. When they got there they looked about and listened. Then, out of the silence of the deep woods, the nightingale began to sing.

"There," said the girl, and she pointed to a small grey bird among the branches.

"Is it possible?" said the Lord Chamberlain. "Why, how common it looks. Perhaps the sight of so many fine people has frightened its colours away."

"Dear Nightingale," he called quite loudly, "I have the honour of commanding you to appear at the palace this evening, where you will charm the Emperor with your wonderful song."

But the nightingale only fluttered to a higher branch. In the end it was the serving girl who finally coaxed the bird to come. And all the way back she carried it cupped in her hands.

The palace had been prepared for the occasion. The walls and floors, all of porcelain, shone with the light of a thousand lamps. Marvelous flowers, hung with golden bells, graced the passageways. And in the centre of the great hall where the Emperor sat, a golden stand had been set up, on which the nightingale was to perch.

The whole court was there dressed in their finest. Even the little serving girl had been given permission to stand by the door and watch. They all fixed their gaze on the little grey bird.

The Emperor nodded and the nightingale began to sing. Its song was so beautiful that tears welled up in his eyes and trickled down his cheeks. And as the bird sang more sweetly still, its song melted the hearts of all who heard.

The nightingale's success was great indeed. From then on it lived at court and had its own cage, and permission to fly out twice a day and once at night. But always there were twelve servants tending it, who each had hold of a silken ribbon tied about its leg. Truly there was not much pleasure in such flights. And when the little serving maid saw the poor bird treated so, it pained her more than words could say.

One day a large parcel came from the Emperor of Japan. On it was written the word *Nightingale*.

"No doubt another book about our famous bird," said the Emperor. But it was not a book. It was a little work of art in a box, a mechanical nightingale cleverly made to resemble the real one, but studded all over with diamonds and sapphires and pearls.

When the bird was wound up, it sang one of the songs that the real nightingale sang and flapped its gold and silver tail in time to the music.

"How wonderful," said everyone. "Now let us hear the two together." But this did not go well, for the real nightingale sang in its own way, while the other bird's song was merely mechanical.

"It's not the new bird's fault," said the Music Master. "It keeps perfect time and sings exactly according to the rules."

So the mechanical bird sang alone. And it was as great a success as the real one, besides being much prettier to look at, for its feathers glittered with precious jewels.

Three and thirty times it sang the same tune and was not the least bit tired. Everyone would gladly have heard it again if the Emperor had not thought it time for the real bird to sing.

But the bird was gone. For while they had been busy with the other, the serving girl had slipped among them and secretly opened the door of its golden cage. And the nightingale had flown unnoticed out the open window, and was on its way back to its own green woods again.

"What is the meaning of this?" cried the Emperor when he saw the empty cage. And he called it a most ungrateful bird. For had he not prized it above all he possessed?

"But we still have the best nightingale," all the courtiers said, attempting to calm the Emperor. Quickly, someone wound the mechanical bird and it sang for the thirty-fourth time.

The Music Master praised the bird to the skies and insisted that it was much better than the real nightingale, not only on the outside with its pearls and precious jewels, but inside as well.

"For you see," he said, "with the real bird, one could never be certain of what was coming next. But with the mechanical bird, everything is prearranged. You can count on things; it will always sing this way and no other. You can open it and watch the works turn and see how one note follows logically on the last."

"Precisely my opinion," agreed the Emperor.

He ordered the Music Master to show the new bird to the public the following day. Everyone 'ohed' and 'ahed' and was much impressed, except for the poor fisherman who had heard the real nightingale.

"It sounds very nice, almost like the real bird," he said, "but still, there is something lacking. I can't say what."

The little nightingale was banished from the kingdom forever, while the clockwork bird was assigned a place of honour on a silken cushion by the Emperor's bed. All around it were arranged the gifts of gold and jewels it had been presented with.

It was given the title of 'High Imperial Court Singer' and the Music Master wrote twenty-five books, full of very long and difficult words, about the bird. Everyone claimed to have read and understood them all, for fear of seeming stupid.

And so it went for a whole year, by which time everyone had learned every note of the bird's song by heart. But they liked it all the better for this, for now they were able to sing along. Only the little serving maid, on her way back from visiting her mother, ever thought to stop in the woods down by the sea, hoping to hear again the nightingale's song.

One night, while the Emperor lay in bed listening to the mechanical bird, something suddenly snapped inside it. There was a loud 'whirr', the wheels spun noisily round and round, and then the music stopped.

The Emperor leapt out of bed and summoned his chief physician. But what could he do? Then the clockmaker was brought in, and after a great deal of discussion and examination, he got the bird to go again. But the pegs were nearly worn, he said, and could not be replaced, so the bird should sing as seldom as possible to save them.

After that the nightingale was wound up only once a year, and even then its song seemed strained, though the Music Master swore it was just as splendid as ever.

Time passed — and then a great sorrow came upon the kingdom. For the Emperor had fallen gravely ill and had taken to his bed. The floors of the palace were covered with felt to muffle the sound of footsteps, and all was silent and still.

The little serving girl brought the news to her mother down by the sea. And on the way back she stopped in the woods where the nightingale once sang.

"Dear little bird," she sighed as she sat beneath the trees. "Though I cannot see you, I feel you are near. I am so sad. The Emperor is ill, and they say that he will surely die. If only you would, you could ease my sadness with your song."

High in the branches overhead there was a rustling of wings. And from the stillness of the green woods, the nightingale began to sing.

Stiff and pale, the Emperor lay in his bed with its long velvet curtains and its great golden tassels. And through the open window the moon shone upon him and upon the mechanical bird by his bed.

He could hardly breathe now; it felt as if there was something sitting on his chest. He opened his eyes and saw that it was Death, wearing his golden crown. In one hand he held the Emperor's sword and in the other the imperial banner. All around him, from between the folds of the heavy curtain about the bed, strange faces peered.

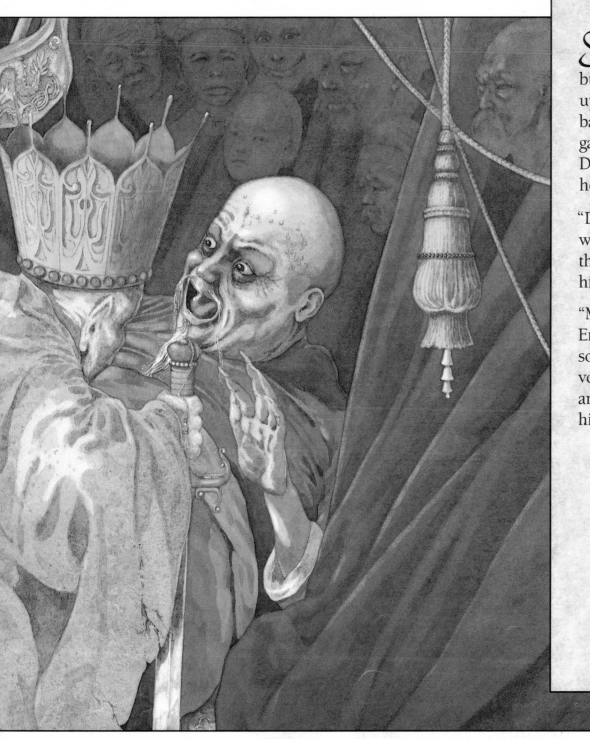

Some were sweet and gentle, but others were horrible to look upon. These were the good and bad deeds of the Emperor, gathered before him now, while Death pressed down upon his heart.

"Do you remember this?" they whispered. "Do you remember that?" And sweat broke out upon his brow at what they said.

"Music! Music!" cried the Emperor. "Let the great drum sound to drown out these voices." But they went on and on, and Death sat solemnly nodding his head all the while.

"Music! Music!" cried the Emperor. "Dear little bird, sing, I beg you. I have given you precious jewels. I have even hung my golden chain about your neck. Now sing, I beg you, sing!"

But the bird stood silent, for it was only mechanical and there was no one to wind it up. And Death kept staring at the Emperor with his great empty eyes as the voices grew louder and more dreadful still.

Then close by the window there was a burst of song. Slowly the Emperor turned his head and saw a small grey bird, perched on a branch outside. The nightingale had come. At its song, the shadows faded and the blood flowed warm in the Emperor's veins. Even Death inclined his head a little and listened.

"Sing, little Nightingale, sing," said Death. And the nightingale sang of the stillness of the graveyard where white roses bloom and lilacs scent the air, and the grass is dewed with the tears of those who mourn for the dead. Thereupon, Death was seized with a longing for his own garden. The sword and banner clattered to the floor, and he crept like a cold grey mist out the window and away.

"Thank you, dear Nightingale," cried the Emperor. "I banished you from my kingdom, yet your song has chased those evil shadows from my bed, and even driven Death himself from my heart." And while the bird went on singing, the Emperor sank into a deep and healing sleep.

The sun was shining in through the window when he awoke, feeling strong and well. None of his attendants had come to him, for they all believed he was dead. But the nightingale still sang.

"Be with me always," said the Emperor, rising from his bed. "I know you cannot be confined to a cage, for you must be free.

But come to me when you can, and in the evening sit upon the branch close by my window. Sing to me of joy and sorrow, and of the good and evil in the world, which are kept hidden from me here. And all will be well, for I will keep you like a close secret, here in my heart. And no one will ever know there is a little bird who tells me everything."

When the attendants came to look upon their dead Emperor, they were amazed. For he stood by the bed in his imperial robes, with his crown on his head and his sword in his hand. And on the floor at his feet, amid scattered pearls and precious jewels, lay the broken remains of the mechanical bird.